James and the Dragon

To/ Sophia,

Happy reading!

Andrew Powell-Thomas 2019

Andrew Powell-Thomas

———————————————————————

James and the Dragon

Illustrations by Harriat King

Olympia Publishers
London

www.olympiapublishers.com
OLYMPIA PAPERBACK EDITION

A CIP catalogue record for this title is
available from the British Library.

ISBN: 978-1-84897-736-5

First Published in 2017
Olympia Publishers
60 Cannon Street London EC4N 6NP

Printed in Great Britain

Dedication

For James

This is the story of a boy named James

and his amazing, incredible rise to fame.

From regular child to hero of the hour,

with cunning and guile as his only power.

The town
where he lived
was a real
friendly place,
all the people
were happy
and had a smile
on their face.

They all worked together and shared all the food, which meant they were always in such a
good mood.

But it didn't last long, for up in the sky,

a dragon appeared with a glint in his eye.

He swooped to the ground
and perched on a tree and he
ate and he ate all the food he
could see.

Day after day the dragon came round,

eating their food and burning the ground.

For the people in town this was no laughing matter,

they were all starving while the dragon got fatter!

"Look out!" they shouted. "He's coming again,

when will this madness ever end?

He's eating our food and destroying our crops,

is there anyone here who can make it all stop?"

Up shot a hand from the back of the crowd.
"I can!" squeaked a voice that wasn't very loud.

Out stepped a man... no, wait... a child!
How can a boy stop a creature so wild?

But he told them his plan and they had to admit,

that it was really quite clever – a definite hit!

"No time to delay, we'll do it tonight,

let's make sure we give that dragon a fright!"

The townsfolk collected their buckets and spades

and they worked and they worked until they made...

A massive hole, the size of a lake,

they filled it with water and then lay in wait.

The very next day the dragon swooped to his tree

and caught sight of something as horrible as could be.

With a long red tail and strange scaly skin,

it had massive front teeth and a real evil grin.

"A monster!" he screamed and started to shake,

trembling with fear his knees did quake.

"That's it! I'm off! It's time to fly!

If I stay round here I'm going to be fried!"

The people shouted, they clapped and they

cheered. "No more living our lives in fear!

Thank goodness he's gone, we've all been saved,

and it's all because of a hero called James!"

James and the Dragon

About the Author

Andrew has been a primary school teacher for ten years. Having taught in West Sussex and abroad, he currently lives in Somerset with his wife, Laura, and young son, James.